The Buddy Files

THE CASE OF THE
LIBRARY MONSTER

Dori Hillestad Butler

Pictures by Jeremy Tugeau and Dan Crisp

Albert Whitman & Company
Chicago, Illinois

Butler, Dori Hillestad.

The Buddy files : the case of the library monster / Dori Hillestad Butler ; illustrated by Jeremy Tugeau and Dan Crisp.

p. cm.

ISBN 978-0-8075-0914-2
[1. Dogs—Fiction. 2. Skinks—Fiction. 3. Libraries—Fiction. 4. Schools—Fiction. 5. Mystery and detective stories.] I. Tugeau, Jeremy, ill II. Crisp, Dan, ill. III. Title. IV. Title: Case of the library monster.

PZ7.B9759Btl 2011

[Fic]—dc22

2010033301

The design is by Nick Tiemersma.

For more information about Albert Whitman & Company, visit our web site at www.albertwhitman.com.

For my friend Amy, who sparked
the idea for this book.

I also owe a huge thank you to Jenni Doll and
Trish Wasek at Witty Kitties in Solon, Iowa.
They know a lot about "monsters."

Table of Contents

1
What Is THAT?

Hello!

My name is Buddy. I'm a therapy dog. That means I get to go to school with Mom and Connor every day. I lie down on a pillow in Mom's office, or here in the library, and people come and

pet me all day long. I LOVE being a therapy dog. It's a very important job!

I'm not just a therapy dog, though. I'm also a detective. A detective is someone who solves mysteries.

There are a lot of mysteries to solve around a school. Right now I'm working on a case I call: The Case of the Four Lakes Elementary School Ghost.

I don't know if there's really a ghost at this school. I don't even know if I believe in ghosts.

Connor believes in ghosts. Connor is my human. He says a girl named Agatha went to school here a long time ago. She got burned in a fire and now her ghost haunts the school.

Here are some reasons I think there could be a ghost here:

- 🐾 I've seen doors close all by themselves.
- 🐾 I've felt cold air ripple through my fur.
- 🐾 And just eleventy-two days ago (or maybe yesterday) I heard strange noises under the floor in the library. Like a ghost was trying to get out!

But all of that could have been caused by:

- 🐾 The wind
- 🐾 My imagination

I've never seen or smelled a ghost before.

Some of Connor's friends say they've seen Agatha. But they weren't telling the truth when they said it. A dog always knows when a human is telling the truth and when a human is lying.

Cat with No Name says he's seen Agatha, too. Unfortunately, there's no way to know if a cat is telling the truth.

But my friend Jazzy also says she's seen the ghost. Jazzy is a dog. Dogs don't lie. If Jazzy says she saw a ghost, then she probably saw a ghost.

Except...I'm still not sure I believe in ghosts.

"Mrs. Christie?" a small voice cuts through my thoughts. "I don't think Buddy is listening."

The voice belongs to a girl who smells like orange juice, toast, peanut butter, and dog. I think Mrs. Warner said the girl's name was Jemma. Mrs. Warner is the alpha human at the library. Mrs. Christie is next in command.

"He's listening," Mrs. Christie says. "Just because he's not sitting up doesn't mean he's not listening."

Mrs. Christie is right.

But so is Jemma. I *wasn't* listening. I was thinking about ghosts.

I'm supposed to listen when kids come to the library to read to me.

It's another one of my jobs at this school.

Mom and Mrs. Warner and Mrs. Christie all say it's good for kids to read to dogs. Especially if those kids aren't good readers. They say kids who read to dogs:

- 🐾 feel more relaxed when they read
- 🐾 Enjoy reading more
- 🐾 Become better readers
- 🐾 Are more willing to read out loud in class
- 🐾 Start doing better in other subjects, too

I feel very good about myself when I hear humans say that.

But there's something Mom,

Mrs. Warner, and Mrs. Christie
don't know about me:

🐾 *I don't know how to read!*

When kids read to me, I don't know if they're getting all the words right. So I just listen. And look at the pictures. Sometimes the pictures tell me if the words are right.

Jemma reads, "empty yellow buses cross the town."

Hmm. I *think* those are yellow buses in that picture. Some colors are hard for me to see. The buses look empty. Unless there are ghosts inside them? And the buses look like they're crossing the town. I think Jemma read those words right.

"You're so smart!" I tell Jemma, licking her cheek. Mmm. Peanut butter! I LOVE peanut butter. It's my favorite food!

Jemma giggles. "Don't lick me!"

She wipes her cheek with her arm, then points to the book in her lap. "Just listen to the story."

"Okay." I rest my chin on her knee.

I like this book. It's all about school buses and what interesting lives they have driving around town, going this way, going that way. It would be fun to be a school bus, I think.

All of a sudden, I hear a strange rustling sound. It's coming from those bookshelves over there.

I raise my head and watch as a book on the bottom shelf slowly slides out of place. Then the book next to it slides out, too. Those books are moving all by themselves.

Maybe there really is a ghost in this school?

Sniff...sniff...sniff. There's a strange smell coming from those shelves. Something I've never smelled before. Is this what ghosts smell like?

"Okay, Jemma," Mrs. Christie says to the girl who's reading to me. "It's time to go back to your class."

"Awww," Jemma groans. "Can't I stay a little longer? I'm almost done with my book."

"I'm sorry," Mrs. Christie says. "We have a special visitor coming this morning, so we need to stop."

"Who's the special visitor?" Jemma asks.

"Bob, the Reptile Guy," Mrs.

Christie replies. "He'll be here any minute, so I have to help Mrs. Warner set up for his visit. And Buddy needs to go back to Mrs. Keene's office."

Yes, but before I go back to the office, I need to find out if there's a ghost hiding in those bookshelves.

Jemma closes her book. "Can I do a trick with Buddy before I go?"

"A quick one," Mrs. Christie says. "Why don't you give him a high five."

I lift my paw and high-five Jemma. Then I yank my leash out of Mrs. Christie's grip and hightail it over to the bookshelves, my leash dragging behind me.

Sniff... sniff... sniff...

Whatever is over there, it's on the

bottom shelf. Behind all those books.

I paw at the books until they drop to the floor and *WHOA!* That's not a ghost hiding in there. It's a MONSTER. A strange, creepy-looking monster!

2
Busted!

For a monster, he's not very big. In fact, he's way smaller than I am. And he doesn't have any fur. He has short, stubby legs with fingers and toes, scaly skin, and a long, skinny, BLUE tongue! I've never met anyone with a tongue like that before.

"Who are you?" I ask, sniffing him. "*What* are you? Where did you come from?"

He stares at me with round little eyes. Man, he smells strange! Sort of like sand... and lettuce... but something else, too.

I notice an open window at the end of the aisle. "Did you crawl in through the window?" I ask.

The monster scurries back behind the books.

"Hey!" I say. More books fall to the floor. "I'm talking to you!"

But that monster is FAST! I climb over the books and stick my head under the shelf so I can see him. *He's climbing up the inside of the shelves!*

"Where are you going?" I ask him. "You can't hide in our bookshelves. Mrs. Warner wouldn't like it."

I hear footsteps behind me. "What

are you barking at, Buddy?" Mrs. Christie asks.

More footsteps. And another voice: "WHAT ARE ALL THOSE BOOKS DOING ON THE FLOOR?"

Uh-oh. That's Mrs. Argus. She's a teacher here. For some reason, she doesn't like me very much.

"I keep telling Mrs. Keene that dogs don't belong in school." Mrs. Argus scowls at the books that are scattered around my feet.

Two or five kids peer around her. I can tell they think I'm a Bad Dog.

"It's not what you think," I tell them. "There's a *monster* hiding in the bookshelves!"

Mrs. Christie smiles. "I wonder if Buddy's found our mouse," she says.

"Mouse!" Mrs. Argus leaps back. I don't think she likes mice any more than she likes me.

"It's not a mouse," I say. "It's a monster. A real, live, blue-tongued monster! He's hiding behind the books. Let me try and get him to come out." I scratch at the books and a few more come tumbling down.

"Okay, okay, Buddy," Mrs. Christie says, grabbing my leash. She bends down and peers between the shelves.

"Do you see him?" I ask, wagging my tail. "Look up between the shelves! That's where he went!"

"Hello?" I hear a man's voice behind me. "Do you ladies work here?"

I turn. Hey, who's *that* guy? Sniff... sniff... and what's inside those cases he's carrying?

Mrs. Christie stands up. "You must be Bob, the Reptile Guy," she says. "I'm Mrs. Christie."

What's a reptile guy? I wonder.

I walk all around him, sniffing him up and down. I thought that monster smelled strange. This guy, and the stuff he's carrying, smells even stranger. Like sand, sticks, water, hot light bulbs, and something else. Something *alive*. There's something alive in *both* of his cases.

The man sets one of the cases on the floor and shakes Mrs. Christie's hand. "Yes, I'm Bob," he says. He offers his hand to Mrs. Argus, too, and she shakes it, but I can tell she doesn't want to.

"We're so happy to have you here," Mrs. Christie says. "Let me introduce you to Mrs. Warner and she can show you where to set up." She leads me and the reptile guy back to the storytime area.

"Uh...what about the monster?"
I ask. We don't want a strange
monster running around loose in the
library, do we?

Of course, I also want to know
what's inside those cases. They smell
so...interesting!

I sniff the case on the floor. I hear
a soft "sssss" sound inside. What is
that?

Sniff...sniff...Is there a *snake* in
that case? I've smelled snakes before,
but I've never actually met one. They
always slither away before I can meet
them. I hope I can meet this one!

"I have quite a bit more to carry
in," Bob says. "Why don't I go get
everything else out of my van and

then you can introduce me to Mrs. Warner."

Mrs. Warner is talking to a group of kids over by the computers, but she hurries over before Bob can leave.

"I'm Mrs. Warner," she says, holding out her hand. "You must be Bob. Thank you for coming today."

Bob shakes her hand. "My pleasure," he says.

"Mrs. Christie, would you help Mrs. Argus's class find some books?" Mrs. Warner asks. "I'll take Bob to the office to meet Mrs. Keene." She turns to Bob. "While we're there, we'll page Mr. Poe. He can help you bring your things in."

"Okay," Bob nods.

"Do you want to take Buddy to the

office with you?" Mrs. Christie asks.

"Sure." Mrs. Warner reaches for my leash.

I groan. I don't want to go back to the office. I want to meet the snake. I want to meet whoever's inside the other case. And I still have to find the monster that's hiding in the bookshelves. I don't think Mrs. Warner even knows there's a monster loose in her library.

"Come on, Buddy," Mrs. Warner says. "No pulling on the leash."

"But … but," I say. But it's no use. Mrs. Warner and the reptile guy walk me to the office.

3
Whoever Heard of a Blue-Tongued Skink?

I sit on my pillow and watch long lines of kids troop past the office. I smell excitement in the air. Those kids must be going someplace fun.

"Stay here, Buddy," Mom says from her desk. "Lie back down on your pillow."

I sigh and lie down. I bet those kids are going to the library. I bet they're going to meet Bob, the Reptile

Guy, his snake, and whatever else he brought. Maybe they'll even see the monster.

I hate that there are interesting things going on in this school without me.

If I listen hard, I can hear kids laughing and clapping and oohing and aahing in the distance. I wish I knew what they were laughing and clapping and oohing and aahing about.

After ten or twenty hours, Mom stands up. She grabs my leash. Oh, boy! I wag my tail. We're going somewhere!

"Ellie?" Mom says to the lady in the main office outside Mom's office. "I'm going to the library. I'd like to catch the end of the reptile presentation."

Oh, boy! The library! I'll get to meet that snake after all.

"Okay," Ellie says. "Do you want to leave Buddy here with me while you go?"

What? NO!

"You don't mind?" Mom asks.

"Not at all," Ellie replies. "Buddy and I are good friends. Would you like a treat, Buddy?"

Treat? I swivel around so I'm facing Ellie. She tosses me a liver treat and I catch it in my mouth. I LOVE liver treats. They're my favorite food! "Would you like another one?" Ellie

reaches into her jar of treats and tosses me another liver treat.

"You bet!" I catch that one in my mouth, too.

"That's all for now," Ellie says, closing up the jar.

"Okay." I turn back to Mom. "Can I please go to the library with you?"

But Mom is already gone.

"So, how was the presentation?" I ask Mom when she comes back a hundred years later. "What did you see? What did you do? Did you meet the snake? Did you see the monster?"

Mom doesn't answer any of my questions. She takes me back to her office and sits down at her desk.

I think she has work to do.

"It's okay," I tell her. "We can talk later."

I turn one, seven, four circles on my pillow and plop down. Work time for Mom means nap time for me. But just as I'm getting settled, the light on the ceiling flickers.

Mom and I both raise our eyes. The light flickers again.

"Are the lights flickering out there?" Mom asks Ellie.

"No," Ellie says. "Are they flickering in your office?"

"Yes," Mom says. "Maybe the bulb is loose." She drags a wooden chair under the light, climbs up, and tightens the bulb.

"Hopefully that'll take care of it," Mom says. Then she goes back to work and I go back to my nap.

After school, Connor stops into the office. His friend Michael is with him. Michael is my friend Mouse's new human. They live on our street.

"Hi, Connor! Hi, Michael!" I say, sniffing them all over. "I'm happy to see you! I'm happy to smell you!" They both smell like … Bob, the Reptile Guy!

"Hi, Buddy," Connor says, scratching my ears. Michael pats my back.

"Mom, can I go over to Michael's house?" Connor asks.

"For a little while," Mom says. And then she says my favorite words: "Do you want to take Buddy with you?"

Please, please, PLEASE say you want to take Buddy with you! I tell Connor with my tail.

"Sure," Connor says. "Buddy likes Michael's dog."

Oh, happy day! I get to go with Connor and Michael. I get to go to Michael's house. I get to visit Mouse.

On the way to Michael's house, Connor and Michael talk about all the animals Bob, the Reptile Guy brought to school. Snakes, tortoises, iguanas, and lizards.

"Which one was your favorite?" Michael asks Connor as we cross a street.

"I liked the bearded dragon. He was cool," Connor says.

"Yeah," Michael agrees. "But I think I liked the lizard with the horns better. I've never seen a lizard like that before."

Connor snorts. "Did you meet Toby Bower before he moved?"

"Is he that kid in Mrs. Adler's class who brought three lizards to school last week?" Michael asks.

"Yeah," Connor says. "He had some of the weirdest lizards I've ever seen. And he had to give them away because his mom said he couldn't take them when they moved. I wonder if he found people to take them all."

Michael shrugs. "I wanted to take

them, but Mrs. Larson wouldn't let me. She said I already have a lizard." He rolls his eyes. "Like a person can only have one lizard."

Michael is what humans call a "foster kid." That means he lives with the Larsons, but he's not really their kid.

"Can I see your lizard?" Connor asks.

"Sure," Michael says.

"I want to see your lizard, too," I say. I've never met a lizard before.

But when we get to Michael's house, Michael and Connor put me in the backyard with Mouse and close the gate.

"HI, BUDDY!" Mouse says, bounding over to me.

"Hi," I say. I let Mouse sniff me as I paw at the fence. "Hey, Connor! Can Mouse and I come in and see Michael's lizard, too?"

Connor doesn't pay any attention. He and Michael go in the house and close the door behind them.

My tail droops.

I shouldn't be surprised. Mouse is an outdoor dog. He hardly ever gets to go inside.

"WHY DO YOU WANT TO SEE MICHAEL'S LIZARD?" Mouse asks. He doesn't mean to yell. He's just so big that when he talks, it sounds like yelling.

"Because I've never seen one before," I say.

"IT ISN'T VERY INTERESTING,"

Mouse says. "AND IT DOESN'T DO MUCH. I DON'T THINK IT CAN EVEN TALK."

"Does it, by any chance, have a blue tongue?" I ask.

"A BLUE TONGUE? I DON'T THINK SO. WHY WOULD YOU ASK THAT?"

I tell Mouse all about the monster in the library.

"STRANGE," Mouse says. "AND YOU DON'T KNOW WHAT THAT MONSTER IS OR WHERE IT CAME FROM?"

"No," I say.

"You dogs are so dumb," says a smug voice in the tree.

I look up. It's Cat with No Name. I don't like it when Cat shows up in the middle of my conversations with Mouse. I *really* don't like it when he calls me dumb.

"There are only about four or five animals in the whole world that have blue tongues," Cat says as he licks his paw. He doesn't tell us what any of those animals are. I think he wants us to ask so he can talk about how dumb we are some more.

"Don't ask," I tell Mouse with my eyes.

He nods at me.

I clench my teeth together. *Don't ask...don't ask*, I tell myself.

But I can't stop myself. "Okay, what animals have blue tongues?" I say really fast. I hate that I said it at all.

Cat jumps to the next branch. "Giraffes and polar bears have bluish-black tongues," he says.

"It wasn't a giraffe or a polar bear," I say.

"WHAT OTHER ANIMAL HAS A BLUE TONGUE?" Mouse asks.

"There are dogs that have blue tongues," Cat says.

He must be talking about Chows. Or Shar Peis. Those dogs have dark tongues. "The Monster I saw was definitely not a dog," I say. "And his tongue was bluer than a Chow's tongue. Or a Shar Pei's tongue. It was bright blue."

"Then it must be a blue-tongued lizard or skink," Cat says. "There are actually six different species of them. They live in Australia."

"IS THIS AUSTRALIA?" Mouse asks.

"No," Cat says, rolling his eyes. "It's Minnesota. I can't stand to be around such dumb dogs." He leaps to the ground, then slips through a hole in the fence.

Mouse and I look at each other.

"I've never heard of a blue-tongued skink," I say.

"ME, EITHER," Mouse says.

"Maybe it's not a real animal," I say. You can't believe everything a cat tells you.

"SOUNDS LIKE YOU HAVE

A NEW CASE TO SOLVE," Mouse says. "THE CASE OF THE LIBRARY MONSTER."

I guess I do.

Here is what I know about the monster so far:

- 🐾 It's small.
- 🐾 It has legs and a tail.
- 🐾 It also has fingers and toes.
- 🐾 Its skin is scaly.
- 🐾 It's fast.
- 🐾 It can climb.

Here is what I don't know about the monster:

- 🐾 What is it?

🐾 Where is it? Is it still in the library or did it go somewhere else?

🐾 Where did it come from?

🐾 Why is it in our school?

Here is what I'm going to do to find out what I don't know:

???

4
I Smell a Monster!

I smell that monster again as soon as Mom opens the door to the school the next day. I run a little bit ahead of her, sniffing...sniffing... sniffing...

I don't think the monster is in this hallway right now, but it's been here. It's been here recently.

Sniff...sniff...sniff...hey, what's that flaky stuff over by the wall?

"Stay with me, Buddy." Mom pulls me closer to her.

"But there's something over there," I say. "Don't you see it?" I think it belongs to the monster. It might be part of its skin. Whoa! *Can this monster actually take his skin off?*

Maybe he's playing a game with me. Maybe he left some skin as a clue and now he wants me to find him.

Mom steers me around the corner. Sniff… sniff… sniff… I don't smell any monsters down this hallway.

"Can we go back the other way?" I ask Mom. "Maybe we should check the library and see if the monster went back in there?"

Mom has no idea what I'm

saying. I'm not sure she even knows I'm trying to talk to her. It's so frustrating when humans don't understand.

Mom leads me into the main office, then into her office, and points to my pillow. "Lie down, Buddy," she says.

I lie down. Mom shuffles over to her desk, turns on her computer, and sits down. The light above her flickers one or seven times. She raises her eyes, sighs, and gets to work.

When Ellie comes in, she says good morning to Mom, then tosses me a treat. Hey, this is a NEW treat. Beef instead of liver. I LOVE beef treats. They're my favorite food!

"Can I please have another one?"

I ask Ellie with my eyes.

The phone rings and Ellie reaches for the phone instead of a treat. "Hello? Four Lakes Elementary School," she says. "Yes…yes…hmm…I don't think so, but I'll check and get back to you."

Ellie hangs up the phone, then calls into Mom's office, "That was Bob, the Reptile Guy on the phone. He thinks he may have left a box of baby mice in the library when he was here yesterday. Do you know if we've found a box of mice?"

"Mice?" Mom's eyebrows rise. "Do you mean *live* mice?"

"That's what it sounds like," Ellie says.

"I doubt it," Mom says. "But check with Mrs. Warner to be sure."

"Okay." Ellie picks up her phone and calls Mrs. Warner. While she's on the phone, Mr. Poe tromps into the main office.

"Hello, Mr. Poe," I say. I like Mr. Poe. He always smells good. Today he smells like wood and oil.

I don't think Mr. Poe sees me lying here in Mom's office. He steps over to the board with all the keys on it. He stares at it for a while, then turns toward Mom's office. "Do you know where the key to the furnace room is, Sarah?" he asks.

"Isn't it hanging on the board?" Mom asks.

"No. It's not," says Mr. Poe.

Mom scoots her chair back and marches over to that board.

I can see from where I'm lying that there's an empty hook on the bottom row. Is there supposed to be a key on that hook?

"That's odd," Mom says, scratching her chin. "If it's not hanging here with the other keys, I don't know where it would be. When was the last time you saw it?"

"I don't know," Mr. Poe says. "I haven't been in the furnace room since last spring. But it's getting colder outside, so I wanted to check the furnace today."

"I noticed that key was missing last week," Ellie says as she hangs up the phone. "I assumed you had it, Mr. Poe. Nobody else ever goes down there."

"I don't have it," Mr. Poe says.

It sounds like there's another mystery to solve around here: The Case of the Missing Key.

All of a sudden, the light in Mom's office flickers and goes out.

Mom groans. "I thought I just had a loose connection in there. Looks like I need a new bulb."

"I'll go get you one," Mr. Poe says.

As soon as he leaves, Mrs. Christie pokes her head into the office. "Are you ready to go to the library, Buddy?" she asks me.

"I'm always ready to go to the library," I say, hopping to my feet. I LOVE the library. It's my favorite place!

Mrs. Christie leads me down the

hall. Sniff...sniff...sniff...*I smell monster!* I also smell pencils, crayons, glue, paint, lots and lots of humans... and as soon as we turn down the hall that leads to the library, I smell monster again! The scent is getting stronger.

Now we're in the library. I'm still sniffing...sniffing...sniffing...where is that monster???

"Do you need to go outside, Buddy?" Mrs. Christie asks. "Maybe I should take you out before the kids come."

"No, I don't need to go outside," I tell Mrs. Christie. "I need to find the monster."

But Mrs. Christie takes me outside anyway. I sigh and quickly do my business. When we get back inside,

I search the library some more.

I don't think the monster is here right now. *So where is he?*

I spend the morning listening to ten or three kids read to me. A lot of the kids bring books about reptiles today instead of books about buses. So now I know what a reptile is.

A reptile:

- 🐾 **Breathes air**
- 🐾 **Is cold-blooded**
- 🐾 **Lays eggs**
- 🐾 **Has skin with scales**
- 🐾 **Is a tetrapod**

"What's a tetrapod?" I ask the kid who's reading to me right now. He smells like sugar, oatmeal, and yuck—

cat! "And what's cold-blooded?"

Sugar-Oatmeal-Cat boy keeps reading: "A tetrapod has four legs or had ancestors with four legs."

"What? Really?" I say. "But I thought a snake was a reptile. Snakes don't have *any* legs."

Thinking about snakes reminds me of Bob, the Reptile Guy, and all the animals he brought. I wonder if the library monster is a reptile? Maybe it belongs to Bob, the Reptile Guy. Maybe it escaped while he was here.

Except, I found the monster before I met Bob, the Reptile Guy. *Didn't I?* Sometimes I have trouble with Before and After.

Also, Bob, the Reptile Guy called

and said he was missing some baby mice. He didn't say anything about missing any reptiles.

"Your time is up, Miles," Mrs. Christie says.

"No, not yet!" I beg. "Tell me why snakes are reptiles. And tell me what cold-blooded means."

Miles shakes my paw. He doesn't answer any of my questions.

He does give me a cracker, though. I LOVE crackers. They're my favorite food!

Then he leaves and somebody else comes to read to me. A girl. She's about Connor's age and she smells like sugar and strawberries... and sniff... sniff... whoa! She also smells like the MONSTER!

5
The Secret Door

Who is this girl and why does she smell like the monster? The smell isn't real strong. Not as strong as it was out in the hallway a little while ago. But it's there on her hands, her stomach, her legs, and her feet.

"Okay, Buddy," Mrs. Christie says, pulling me away from the girl. "Let's let Maya get settled."

Maya giggles as she drops to her knees beside me. She hugs a book to her chest.

Mrs. Christie loosens her grip on my leash and I sniff Maya's shoulders and her neck.

"I think he likes you," Mrs. Christie tells Maya.

But I'm not sniffing Maya because I like her. I'm sniffing her for clues. Clues to who she is, why she smells like the monster, and where the monster might be.

Unfortunately, I don't smell any clues.

"Okay, Buddy," Mrs. Christie says. "Time to lie down." She points at the floor.

I lie down close to Maya.

Maya gives me a little pat, then shows me her book. "It's called *Blue-Tongued Skink*," she says.

Blue-tongued skink? I can hardly believe my ears. Or my eyes. There, on the cover, is a picture of the monster I saw in this very library!

So a blue-tongued skink *is* a real animal. Cat with No Name didn't make it up.

Maya opens the book and starts reading. I sit up so I can see the pictures better.

"Did you know you smell like one of those?" I ask her.

Maya doesn't answer. She just keeps reading.

"I think it's very interesting that you smell like a blue-tongued skink and you're reading a book about them," I tell her.

"Buddy, shh!" Mrs. Christie says, putting her finger to her lips.

But I can't shh! I have too much to say.

"Did you know there's one of those guys somewhere in this school?" I ask. "I saw him in the library. I smelled him in the hallway. I don't know where he is now. Can you help me find him?"

Maya doesn't understand a word I'm saying.

I sigh. If I can't talk to Maya, maybe I should listen to her read. Maybe she'll read something that will give me a clue to finding the blue-tongued skink.

I start to lie down when Maya reads, "A blue-tongued skink can be a very nice pet."

I sit back up. *It can?* "Do you have a blue-tongued skink at your house?" I ask Maya. "Is that why you smell like one?"

"Buddy!" Mrs. Christie says. She turns to Maya. "I don't know why he's barking so much today."

"Maybe he needs to go outside?" Maya suggests.

"Maybe," Mrs. Christie says. "Though I just put him out half an hour ago."

"I DON'T NEED TO GO OUT-SIDE!" I yell. "I NEED TO FIGURE SOME THINGS OUT."

I lie back down so I can think.

And so Mrs. Christie stops wondering if I need to go outside.

The reason Maya smells like a blue-tongued skink could be that she has one for a pet. If she does, it's probably not the same one I found here at school. Her blue-tongued skink is probably at her house.

Unless it escaped and came to our school?

No. If that had happened, Maya would smell worried right now. She doesn't smell worried; she smells happy.

"Blue-tongued skinks do not lay eggs like other reptiles," Maya goes on. "They give birth to live young."

Other reptiles? So a blue-tongued skink *is* a reptile.

Maya turns a page. "Blue-tongued skinks are cold-blooded," she reads. "They can't control their own body temperature. Your tank should have a heater and a basking light."

While Maya reads, I make a list inside my head of everything I am learning about blue-tongued skinks:

- 🐾 They don't lay eggs.
- 🐾 They need heat.
- 🐾 They need light.
- 🐾 They need water.
- 🐾 They like to hide.
- 🐾 Their skin comes off in little pieces.
- 🐾 They eat fruit, vegetables, canned dog food (!!!!), and mice.

None of that information helps me figure out where the blue-tongued skink came from, why he's in our school, or where he might be now.

I spend the rest of the day thinking about that blue-tongued skink. Now I'm back in Mom's office. School is out. Mom and Ellie are still here, but all the kids have gone home. This would be a good time to go sniff around the rest of the school.

But I'm supposed to stay here on this pillow. Mom told me to stay.

Mom is typing away at her computer. Ellie is talking to someone on the phone. I could probably sneak away. I wouldn't have to be gone long.

Maybe I could get back before Mom even noticed I was gone.

But when Mom tells me to stay, I'm supposed to stay. That's the rule.

Well... sometimes a dog has to break the rules.

With one eye on Mom and Ellie, I keep my body low to the ground... and creeeeeep past Ellie's desk, around the corner, and out into the hallway.

Safe!

Then I put my nose to the ground and sniff. I don't smell anything unusual in this hall... or this hall... or this hall... I go down some stairs... hey, I've never been in this part of the school before.

There are no classrooms down

here. Just a dark hallway that smells musty. And some closed doors. It's kind of scary down here, a place a ghost would hang out. If there was one at this school.

Suddenly, I hear footsteps on the stairs behind me. Slow, quiet footsteps.

I freeze.

There's no place to run. No place to hide.

Oh! No worries. It's *Maya* on the stairs.

"Oh!" she says when she sees me. She is as surprised to see me as I am to see her.

I wag my tail. "What are you doing here?" I ask. "I thought all the kids went home."

She puts her finger to her lips. "Shh!" she says.

I trot along beside her. "Where are we going?" I ask.

She doesn't answer.

We stop in front of one of the closed doors. There's a sign on the door, but I can't read the words on the sign.

Maya reaches into her pocket and pulls out a key. She smells nervous.

"What are you doing?" I ask her with my eyes.

She glances all around. But it's just her and me down here.

I watch as she unlocks the door. She only opens it wide enough so she can squeeze through.

"What's in there?" I ask, trying to nose my way in. "Can I come in, too?"

The door slams closed in my face.

6
Stay!

I sniff the crack under the door.
I smell dirt, dust, mold. What's in
that room? It doesn't smell like stuff
you normally smell around a school.
"Maya!" I scratch at the door.
"Come back. Let me in."
I don't think she can hear me.
I sniff some more. Now I smell
spiders...mice...old books...paint.

"What are you doing in there?"
I ask. I wonder if she's supposed to
be in there. Well, she had a key. She
probably wouldn't have a key if she
wasn't supposed to be in there.

I press my ear against the door
and listen. I hear banging. I also
hear things moving around. Big
things. Heavy things.

Then I hear Maya cry out. "Oh,
no," she says. "No! No! No! No! No!"

Uh-oh. That doesn't sound good.
I scratch at the door again. "Maya?
What's wrong?" I sure wish I could
open this door.

There's a voice behind me.
"What are you doing all the way
down here, Buddy?" Mr. Poe asks.
"Does Mrs. Keene know you're

running around loose?"

"I don't know," I say. "That's not important. What's important is Maya's in there! I think she could be in trouble."

Mr. Poe grabs hold of my leash and moves me away from the door.

"Wait!" I say, digging my paws into the floor. "We have to help Maya!"

But the floor is slippery. And Mr. Poe is STRONG. He pulls me across the floor...up the stairs...around the corner...down the hall...all the way back to the office.

Ellie raises her head when we walk in. She draws in her breath. "I didn't know Buddy was loose, did you, Sarah?"

"No!" I hear Mom before I see her. She comes out to Ellie's office and takes my leash from Mr. Poe. "Thanks for finding him. He's usually much better about staying on his pillow." She looks at me like I am a Bad Dog.

"No problem," Mr. Poe says. "Now if only I could find that key to the furnace room as easily as I found your dog."

"I'll call the former principal of this school and see if she has any idea where it might be," Mom says, leaning against the door jamb. "If not, I'll call a locksmith to come and unlock that door. We've got to get in there and check the furnace pretty soon."

Mr. Poe nods. "Sounds good," he says. Then he leaves.

Mom points to my pillow. "Lie down, Buddy," she says.

I go and lie down.

"And *stay* this time," Mom says, returning to her desk.

I stay. Even though I really, really, really want to know what Maya is up to. Is she in trouble? Does anyone know where she is?

After ten or a hundred minutes, I hear footsteps in the hallway. Running footsteps.

Ellie gets up and goes out into the hall. "No running," she says.

The running footsteps become walking footsteps. A small voice says, "Sorry."

Maya? I sit up.

"Down!" Mom says.

I lie back down. I'm pretty sure that was Maya's voice I heard. That means she's out of the secret room. That's good. But why would she run down the hall? Where is she going in such a hurry?

I hear the door to the playground open and close. I can't quite see out Mom's window when I'm lying down, so I stretch my neck as high as I can and watch Maya zoom across the playground.

She calls out to a group of boys who are playing football in the grass. Mom's window is closed so I can't hear what she's saying. But I see a boy stop and turn toward Maya. He's

a little older than she is. She motions
for him to come over to her.

It's too hard to see like this, so I sit
all the way up. I watch Maya's hands
move in big circles. Whatever she's
telling him must be very important.
Then they race toward the school.

"Buddy!" Mom says.

I drop to my belly.

"STAY!" Mom says.

"Okay, okay," I say. There's nothing
to see outside right now anyway.

I hear an outside door open and
close again. It must be Maya and that
boy. I wait, but they don't ever pass by
the office. Are they really inside the
school?

I listen. I sniff. I don't hear or
smell anything unusual.

After fifty-eleven minutes, Ellie says goodbye and leaves.

"Stay," Mom says to me again. Even though I have not gotten up.

Finally, after seventy-twelve more minutes, Mom turns off her computer and reaches for her keys. We must be leaving soon.

"Okay, Buddy," Mom says.

That means I can get up!

Mom picks up my leash, turns out the lights in her office and the main office, and locks the main office door behind us. As we move down the hall, I am sniffing...sniffing...sniffing. But I can't tell whether Maya and that boy are inside the school or not.

Outside I see my friend Jazzy snoozing in her backyard. Jazzy is a pug. She and I met at obedience school a long, long time ago when I helped her and our other friend Muffin get back to their real humans.

"Jazzy!" I call.

She raises her head. "Buddy! Hi!" She scampers to the fence to greet me. Mom is not heading to the fence; she's heading toward the car.

"Did you see a girl that smells like strawberries and sugar?" I ask Jazzy over my shoulder. That's the best way to describe Maya. The strawberries and sugar smell is much stronger than the monster smell. "She was out here a little while ago. She was talking to a boy."

"Do you mean Maya? Yes, I saw her. She was talking to her brother,

Alex," Jazzy says.

I wag my tail. "You know them?"

Mom opens the back door for me. "Hop up," she says.

I pretend I don't know what Mom wants me to do. "Did you hear what Maya said to her brother?" I ask Jazzy.

"Something about mice," Jazzy says.

"What about them?" I ask.

"I don't know," Jazzy says.

"Did you hear them say anything else?"

Jazzy thinks for a minute. "She also said Felix, Freckles, and Fluffy are gone!"

"Who are Felix, Freckles, and Fluffy?" I ask.

"I have no idea," Jazzy says.

7
Locked In

"Let's go, Buddy," Mom says. "In the car." She pats the back seat. But I am in the middle of a very important conversation.

"Where are Maya and Alex now?" I ask Jazzy.

"I don't know," she says. "I saw them go in that door over there." She tips her head toward the far door at the end of the school. "I don't think they ever came out."

I have to find out what Maya and Alex are up to. I yank my leash out of Mom's grasp and RUN for that door.

"Buddy!" Mom stomps her foot. "Come back here!"

I keep running. Along the way I pick up Maya's scent. Her brother's scent, too.

I can feel Mom chasing me across the playground. I know she isn't happy. But I have to follow Maya and Alex's trail. I follow it all the way to the school. Unfortunately, the door is closed.

I don't know why all buildings can't have a doggy door like I have at my house.

I peer in through the glass. Mr. Poe is mopping the floor.

"Let me in!" I say, scratching at the slippery door. "Please, let me in!"

Mr. Poe comes over and pushes the door open with his hip.

"Grab him!" Mom yells to Mr. Poe. "Grab Buddy!"

Mr. Poe reaches for me, but I leap away before he can grab me. I charge across the wet floor. Sniffing... sniffing... sniffing. Uh-oh. I think Mr. Poe has mopped away Maya and Alex's trail.

No, wait. When I get to a part of the floor where Mr. Poe hasn't mopped yet, I pick up the trail again. I follow it down the hall, around the corner, around another corner, down the stairs, all the way to that secret door.

I sniff the door. I don't hear voices or anything moving around inside, but I'm pretty sure I smell those kids in there.

"BUDDY, SIT!" Mom yells

as she hurries toward me. "SIT AND STAY!"

I sit.

"Good boy," Mom says, grabbing my leash.

I pop back up and scratch at the door some more. "PLEASE OPEN THIS DOOR!" I say. "Maya and Alex are in there. We have to find out what they're doing."

"What does Buddy want in the furnace room?" Mom asks.

This is the furnace room?

"I don't know," Mr. Poe says. "He must smell something. I wish we could get in there." He tries the door, but it's locked.

"Without a key, there isn't much we can do," Mom says. "Come on, Buddy. Let's go home."

Hmm. I think I have yet *another* new case. On the way home, I think about The Case of Maya, the Missing Key, and the Furnace Room.

Here is what I know about my new case:

- 🐾 Maya and Alex were in the furnace room.
- 🐾 Mr. Poe and Mom don't know where the key to the furnace room is.
- 🐾 Maya had a key to the furnace room.

I think Maya took the key. But why would she do that?

There are more things that I *don't* know about this new case than there are things that I do know. Here is what I don't know:

- 🐾 Why was Maya in the furnace room?

- 🐾 Why does she have a key to the furnace room?
- 🐾 Why did she say, "No! No! No! No! No!" when she was in there?
- 🐾 Who are Felix, Freckles, and Fluffy?
- 🐾 Where did Felix, Freckles, and Fluffy go?
- 🐾 What do mice have to do with anything?
- 🐾 Why did Maya and her brother run back into the school?

Here is what I'm going to do to find out what I don't know:

Maybe I should go back to the Case of the Library Monster. Or the case of the Four Lakes Elementary School Ghost. But I don't have a plan for figuring out how to solve either of those cases, either.

Sometimes being a detective is hard.

The next morning when Mom, Connor, and I arrive at school, I spy Alex on the playground. He's playing basketball with some other boys. I don't see Maya.

Connor has hold of my leash because Mom is getting something out of the trunk. It's a BIG box. But not a very deep box. It doesn't smell very interesting.

"Can I go play basketball with those boys?" I ask Mom as she slams the trunk.

"I think Buddy wants to play on the playground, Mom. Is that okay?" Connor asks.

Did Connor understand me?

"That's fine," Mom says. "As long as you bring him to the office when the bell rings."

Connor and I join the basketball game.

I stick close to Alex. He smells like dog and rabbit and bacon and eggs. He does not smell like blue-tongued skink. If Maya has a blue-tongued skink for a pet, Alex must not spend much time with it.

I follow Alex all around the basketball court. I sniff. I listen. I watch. But I don't learn anything that will help me solve any of my mysteries.

The bell rings and all the kids run toward the school. Connor brings me to the office. I go on ahead of him and plop down on my pillow. I'm exhausted.

Connor doesn't come in. Instead, he PUTS A GATE across Mom's doorway.

"Hey! What are you doing?" I charge toward the gate. It doesn't budge.

I rest my chin on top of the gate and peer at Connor. "Did you know you just locked Mom and me in her office?"

Connor looks a little sorry. "See you later, Buddy," he says with a wave.

I gaze over at Ellie. She makes sad eyes at me, then reaches into her treat jar and tosses me a beef treat. I catch it in my mouth. I love beef treats, but they don't make me feel any better about that gate.

"I'm sorry we had to put up a gate, Buddy," Mom says. "But we can't have you running around loose in the school."

"I only run around loose in the school when I have something important to do," I tell her.

At least I am only stuck behind that gate for eleventy-two minutes. Then Mrs. Christie comes to get me.

"Oh, boy!" I say, hopping to my feet. "Time to read!" I wonder if Maya will read to me today. Or Alex.

As Mrs. Christie and I turn a corner, I pick up a trail. I smell blue-tongued skink! He's still around. But where is he?

I am sniffing ... sniffing ... sniffing ...

Darn. I lost the trail.

"This way, Buddy." Mrs. Christie steers me into the library.

I can't tell whether Blue-Tongued Skink has been back to the library or not. And there's no time to explore because there's already a kid sitting on my pillow when I get there. He waves at me and Mrs. Christie.

"Hi, Noah," Mrs. Christie says as

we settle in on the pillow.

Noah smells like cereal and milk. I LOVE cereal and milk. They're my favorite foods! Noah reads to me about things that go up and down. Then I play dead for him and he goes back to his class.

The next kid reads about a boy named Henry, a dog named Mudge, and a very dirty cat. The parts about the cat are boring, but I like Mudge. He reminds me of my friend Mouse.

Another kid reads to me about snakes. And the kid after that reads to me about lizards.

Just when I think I'm not going to see Maya today (or ever again), she strolls into the library.

I wag my tail. "Hi, Maya," I say.

"Are you going to read to me?"

"Hi, Buddy," she says. She's smiling with her mouth, but not her eyes.

"Look what I brought." Maya shows me that same book she brought last time. The one with the blue-tongued skink on the cover. I note that she doesn't smell very much like blue-tongued skink today. She sits down on the pillow next to me and Mrs. Christie and starts to read.

I have a hard time keeping my mind on Maya's book because Maya smells worried. Worried or scared. It's hard to tell.

"What's the matter, Maya?" I ask. "Why are you worried? Why are you scared?"

She keeps reading.

"Does it have something to do with the furnace room?" I ask.

Maya turns a page, rubs my back, and keeps on reading.

"Who are Felix, Freckles, and Fluffy? Did you ever find them?" I ask.

Maya doesn't answer my questions. When she finishes reading, Mrs. Warner says, "You're the last reader this morning, Maya. Would you like to take Buddy back to the office?"

"Okay," Maya says.

Maya doesn't answer my questions when we're alone in the hall, either. She just pets me and tells me what a good dog I am.

Mom opens the gate and lets me into her office. "Thanks, Maya," she says, closing the gate behind me.

"You're welcome," Maya replies.

Then something very strange happens. Mom goes back to her desk and Maya tiptoes over to that board with all the keys.

She peers over her shoulder, hangs a key on the empty hook, and scurries toward the door.

8
What Did Maya Do?

Ellie wanders into the office as Maya is trying to leave. The two nearly run into each other in the doorway.

"Excuse me, dear," Ellie says as she scoots around Maya. She stops in front of the gate. "Have you called the locksmith about the furnace room lock yet?" she asks Mom.

"No, I forgot. I'll do that right

now," Mom says. She reaches for the phone.

"You don't have to call anyone," I tell Mom. "The key is back!"

"Shh, Buddy," Mom says, putting her finger to her mouth. "I'm on the phone."

I lie down on my pillow and listen as she makes plans for someone to come and open the furnace room door and put in a new lock next Thursday.

I sigh. Nobody ever listens to the dog.

Eleventy-seven minutes later, Mr. Poe strolls into the office. He stops in front of the board with the keys. "Hey, you found the key to the furnace room," he says.

"No," Mom says. "But I called a

97

locksmith. They'll be out next week."

"The key's right here," Mr. Poe says, taking it off the hook.

"Really?" Mom stands up. "That's strange. Well, I'm glad it's back. Are you going to check the furnace today?"

"I'll do it right now," Mr. Poe says.

I go to the gate. "Can I go with you?" I ask, wagging my tail. I'd really like to see what's in that furnace room.

Mr. Poe leaves without answering me.

I guess that's a no.

The good thing about the gate in Mom's office is I don't have to be on a leash when I'm in her office. And

I don't have to stay on my pillow. I can sit by the window and see what's happening on the playground.

I like to watch the birds and the squirrels and the kids at recess. Hey, Maya and Alex are outside. They're not playing; they're talking quietly over by that tree. I wonder what they're talking about. Whatever it is, it looks serious.

I think I'd like to go outside now. I let out a little woof, but Mom doesn't look up.

I woof again. Louder this time. Then I turn a circle in front of Mom's desk. That gets her attention.

"Do you need to go outside, Buddy?" she asks.

"Yes! Yes! Yes!" I say.

The light above us flickers. Mom squints up at it and sighs. "I guess that light still isn't fixed," she says. Then she clips my leash to my collar, moves the gate, and hurries me outside.

Connor is outside, too. He's talking to some kids on the climbing toy across the playground. But he waves when he sees us.

"Connor?" Mom calls. "Will you bring Buddy to the office when recess is over?"

"Okay," he says. He slides down the slide and runs toward us. Mom unhooks my leash and I AM FREE! I give Connor a quick lick, then say, "Sorry, Connor. I can't play right now."

I dash across the playground toward Maya and Alex. But Alex is backing away from Maya now.

"What do you think I should do?" Maya cries.

Alex shrugs. "I don't know," he says. "You should never have taken them in the first place."

Taken what?

"This is your problem, not mine," Alex says. Then he heads off to join a group of kids playing football.

Maya plops down on the grass and leans back against a tree. She looks glum.

I lie down beside her and rest my head on her knee. "What's the matter, Maya?" I ask.

"Hi, Buddy," Maya says. She pats

my head. "I did something I shouldn't have done."

"What?" I ask. "What did you do?"

"First I stole a key from the office," Maya says. "Then I took it to the hardware store and made a copy of it. Then—I can't even tell you what I did after that!" She buries her face in her hands.

The bell rings. Maya dries her eyes on her sleeve.

"Buddy?" Connor calls. "Where are you? Ah, there you are! Come here, boy." He pats his legs.

"I'll see you later, Buddy," Maya says as she drags herself to her feet.

What could she possibly have done that would make her feel so bad?

Mr. Poe lumbers into the office right behind Connor and me.

"I hear you're still having some trouble with that light," Mr. Poe says.

Connor leads me into Mom's office, then slides the gate across the doorway. I go lie on my pillow.

Mom sighs. "Yes. I don't know what the problem could be. The lights aren't flickering anywhere else in the school. And you've already replaced the bulb."

"Could be a short in the wire. Or," Mr. Poe's eyes twinkle. "Maybe we have a ghost."

Mom scowls. "There's no such thing as ghosts, Mr. Poe," she says.

"Are you sure about that?" Mr. Poe asks.

"Please just fix the light," Mom says.

Hmm. I've been worrying so much about that blue-tongued skink and about Maya's problems that I completely forgot about the ghost! Was a ghost making Mom's light flicker?

After school, Connor goes over to Mouse's house again. I'm glad he and Michael are getting to be such good friends. And I'm glad he lets me come along to play with Mouse, even if they go in the house and don't play with us.

"HAVE YOU CAUGHT THE LIBRARY MONSTER YET?" Mouse asks me.

"No," I say. "But I found out what it is. It's a blue-tongued skink, just like Cat said."

"HOW DO YOU KNOW?" Mouse asks.

"I saw a picture of it in a book that a kid read to me," I say. "But that's not the only thing going on at the school right now."

I tell Mouse about Maya and Alex, and about them going into the furnace room, and what Jazzy overheard about mice, and about Felix, Freckles, and Fluffy being gone, and the fact that Maya did something she shouldn't have done. I also tell him about the flickering light in Mom's office.

"I keep finding new mysteries to solve before I can solve all the old mysteries." I drop to my belly and rest my chin on my paws.

"MAYBE THEY AREN'T ALL NEW MYSTERIES," Mouse says. "MAYBE THEY'RE ALL PART OF THE SAME MYSTERY, AND YOU JUST HAVE TO FIND OUT HOW THOSE MYSTERIES FIT TOGETHER."

"I don't know," I say. "What does a blue-tongued skink have to do with a flickering light?"

"MAYBE NOTHING," Mouse says. "BUT MAYBE SOMETHING."

"And what does Maya sneaking into the furnace room have to do with the missing Felix, Freckles, and Fluffy?" I ask.

"MAYBE NOTHING," Mouse says. "BUT MAYBE SOMETHING."

"It would help if I knew who Felix, Freckles, and Fluffy were," I say.

"OR WHAT THEY WERE," Mouse puts in.

What could they be? Humans? Animals? Aliens from outer space?

"Jazzy overheard Maya and Alex talking about baby mice. Maybe Felix, Freckles, and Fluffy are mice?" I say.

"MAYBE," Mouse says.

Bob, the Reptile Guy was missing some mice. Did Maya take them? Is that what she meant when she said she did something she shouldn't have done? Did she steal the mice? Did she hide them in the furnace room?

Then I remember something Maya read in that book. Something

that makes my fur stand straight up. *Blue-tongued skinks EAT mice.* And there's a blue-tongued skink in our school!

9
Before It's Too Late

"YOU HAVE TO FIND BLUE TONGUE, BUDDY," Mouse says. "YOU HAVE TO FIND HIM BEFORE HE EATS FELIX, FRECKLES, AND FLUFFY."

"I know," I say. "But how can I do that when there's a gate in Mom's office?"

"CAN YOU JUMP OVER THE GATE?" Mouse asks.

"Maybe," I say. "But Mom will chase me. The whole school will probably chase me."

"THEN YOU'LL HAVE TO FIND BLUE TONGUE BEFORE THEY CATCH YOU," Mouse says.

Where could Blue Tongue be?

I've seen him in the library. I've seen pieces of his skin in the hall by the main door. But that doesn't mean I'll find him in the library or the hall.

Where would *I* go if I were loose in a school? I'd go where the food is: the lunchroom.

But Blue Tongue is a reptile. He might go someplace different.

I think back over everything I know about blue-tongued skinks. Maybe I know something that will help me find him. Here is what I know:

- 🐾 **Their skin comes off in little pieces.**
- 🐾 **They like to hide.**
- 🐾 **They need light.**
- 🐾 **They need heat because they can't control their own body temperature.**

Uh-oh. Eleventy-eight minutes ago I was worried about the mice. Now I'm worried about Blue Tongue, too. What if the school isn't warm enough for him? What will happen to him if he gets too cold? I have to find him. Before it's too late.

Where is the warmest place in the school? I wonder as Mom and I make our way toward the office the next day. If Blue Tongue is smart, he'll be hiding in a very warm place.

We walk past a heater, but there isn't any air blowing out of it.

Sniff... sniff... hey, I think I smell Blue Tongue! I also smell pancakes, sausage, butter, and maple syrup. I LOVE pancakes, sausage, butter, and maple syrup. They're my favorite foods!

But I smell Blue Tongue, too. Really, I do! I think he's in the cafeteria with the kids who are eating breakfast.

I pull Mom toward the cafeteria.

"Whoa, Buddy," she says, holding

tight to the leash. "Where are we going?"

"In here."

"Hi, Mrs. Keene! Hi, Buddy!" a bunch of kids wave to us from the tables.

Sniff… sniff… sniff… hmm, I don't think Blue Tongue is in *here* exactly. But he could be in the kitchen! Where there's even more pancakes, sausage, butter, and maple syrup.

I give my leash a hard tug and pull it out of Mom's hand. Then I race toward the kitchen.

"Buddy!" Mom calls, hurrying after me. But I'm faster than she is.

"No dogs in the kitchen!" one of the cooks says. She claps her hands and chases me around a big table.

Sniff... sniff... sniff... I definitely smell Blue Tongue! He's in here somewhere. But where?

"If you can't catch Buddy, step on his leash," Mom says to the cook. Now they're both chasing me around the table.

Hey, a stove is a warm place. Maybe Blue Tongue is over there.

I dart under the table and over to the stove. Sniff... sniff... sniff... YES! I smell him! Blue Tongue is under the stove! I stretch my front paw as far as I can, but I can't reach him.

"Come on out of there," I say. "You don't belong under the stove."

"What is that crazy dog doing?"

one of the cooks asks.

"Maybe he smells a mouse," the other cook says.

"Not a mouse," I say. "A skink. A blue-tongued skink!"

Mom snatches my leash and tries to drag me away from the stove, but I won't let myself be dragged away. Not this time. I paw and bite at the stove. "We have to get under there!" I tell Mom and the cooks. "We have to get that skink!"

"Should we move the stove and see what Buddy is so interested in?" one of the cooks asks.

"Yes! Move the stove," I say, backing away a little to give them room.

One of the cooks grabs one end.

Another cook grabs the other end. They count, "One, two, three" and pull the stove out from the wall.

"Careful," I say, peering underneath. "Don't squish Blue Tongue!"

I can see him under there. He isn't squished. But he isn't moving, either.

"What's back there?" one of the cooks asks. They both peer over the top of the stove.

"I don't know," the other cook says. "I don't see anything."

"That's because he's still mostly under the stove," I say. "Excuse me. Excuse me." I nose the cooks out of the way and squeeze back behind the stove.

"Hello?" I nudge Blue Tongue with my nose.

He doesn't say anything.
"Are you okay?" I ask.
I think he's okay. His eyes are open. He's breathing. And his body feels warm against my nose.
I nudge him again.

All of a sudden he scoots through that opening between the stove and the counter. He's out into the kitchen now.

A bunch of people in the kitchen SCREAM!

"WHAT IS IT?" yells one of the cooks.

"I DON'T KNOW," yells another cook. "SOMEONE CALL MR. POE!"

"No, don't call Mr. Poe," I say, squeezing out from behind the stove. I take off after Blue Tongue. "I'll catch him!" He may be fast, but I'm faster!

I chase Blue Tongue across the kitchen and into the lunchroom where all the kids are eating breakfast. Blue Tongue stops, turns, and scurries along the wall. I stay with him ... all the way to the corner. Now he's stuck!

"I've got him," I call over my shoulder.

"Hey, Buddy's got something," one of the kids says.

"What does he have?" someone else asks. A bunch of kids surround me.

"Whoa! What is that?"

In the distance I hear somebody whisper, "Oh, no! It's Fluffy."

10
Questions and Answers

Fluffy?

Who said that? Maya? She and Alex are standing at the edge of the crowd, shushing each other.

I stare at Blue Tongue. THIS is Fluffy?

Fluffy isn't a mouse? He's a blue-tongued skink? Who would name a blue-tongued skink Fluffy? Well...who would name a big, black dog Mouse? There's no understanding humans sometimes.

So what about Felix and Freckles? Felix and Freckles must not be mice either. Are they blue-tongued skinks, too? Is there more than one blue-tongued skink in this school?

"What have you got there, Buddy?" Mom asks, making her way through the crowd. Mrs. Warner and Mrs. Argus are right on her heels. "Oh!" Mom says when she sees what I have. "What is that thing?"

"It's a blue-tongued skink," Mrs. Warner says. She picks Fluffy up and cradles him in her arms.

Several kids crowd in to pet him, even though he doesn't have any fur.

"Where did he come from?" Mrs.

Warner asks.

"Buddy found him in the kitchen," Mom says. "I don't know how he got there."

I turn to Maya and Alex. I don't know exactly how Fluffy got here, either. But I can tell by the way Maya is biting her lip and Alex is shifting his weight from one foot to the other that they both know something about all of this.

I wonder if this is what Maya was hiding in the furnace room. But why would she hide a blue-tongued skink in the furnace room at school?

"What are you going to do with him, Mrs. Warner?" one of the kids asks.

"Call Animal Control," Mrs.

Argus says, wrinkling her nose. "Whatever it is, it clearly doesn't belong here."

"I think you should put him in the library. Yeah, put him in the library," several kids suggest.

"I've got an empty aquarium in my classroom," one of the teachers says, slipping away from the crowd. "You can put him in there until you decide what to do with him."

"Thank you, Mrs. Sobol," Mrs. Warner calls after her. She turns to the rest of the group. "I'm not going to call Animal Control. This guy must belong to someone. I'll place a lost and found ad in the newspaper and see if anyone claims him."

Mrs. Sobol returns with an

empty aquarium and Mrs. Warner carefully sets Blue Tongue inside.

"I know it's no fun being locked up," I tell Blue Tongue. "But trust me. You're better off in there than you are running around loose in the school. The humans will feed you and make sure you stay warm enough. They may even take you out and play with you now and then."

I wait for Blue Tongue to thank me for finding him, but he just sticks his skinny blue tongue out at me.

The bell rings. Mrs. Warner carries the aquarium away. The kids all go to their classes. And Mom takes me to the office.

I go over to my pillow, turn around, and plop down. It's been a

busy morning!

I should be happy. I found Fluffy before he got too cold.

I also have answers to a lot of my questions.

I know what the monster is:

🐾 **He's a blue-tongued skink.**

I THINK I know where he came from:

🐾 **I think Maya was hiding him in the furnace room.** .

And if I'm right about that, then I can also guess why Maya took the key out of the case:

🐾 **Because she was hiding Felix, Freckles, and Fluffy in the furnace room.**

But there are still a lot of things
I don't know:

- 🐾 Why did Maya hide a blue-tongued skink in the furnace room?
- 🐾 What about Felix and Freckles? What are they? Are they blue-tongued skinks, too?
- 🐾 Where are Felix and Freckles?
- 🐾 How did Fluffy get from the furnace room to the library?
- 🐾 What about the mice? Jazzy heard Maya talking

about mice. And Bob, the
Reptile Guy is missing some
mice. Where are the mice?

🐾 Why didn't Maya tell anyone
Fluffy belongs to her?

And here is the thing I'm wondering about most:

🐾 Did I solve the Case of the
Library Monster or not?

Later on, Mrs. Warner comes into the office. She knocks on Mom's door. "Look what somebody left on my desk," she says, holding up a piece of paper with typed words on it.

Mom looks up from her computer.

"A note? What does it say?"

Mrs. Warner reads, "Dear Mrs. Warner. Thank you for finding Fluffy. If you go in the girls' bathroom by Mrs. Nixon's room, you'll find Fluffy's friends, Felix and Freckles. I got them from a friend who moved away. I thought my mom would let me keep them, but she said they couldn't be in the house. So I found a new place to keep them. A SECRET place. But then they all escaped. I found Felix and Freckles right away, but I didn't know where Fluffy was until Buddy found him. I don't think the secret place is a good place for lizards. Can you please keep them in the library? Then everyone can enjoy them. Signed, Anonymous."

"Hmm," Mom says.

"I went into that bathroom," Mrs. Warner says. "There was another aquarium with two lizards in it and a box with some baby mice for food. Remember Bob, the Reptile Guy was missing a box of baby mice?"

Mom leans back in her chair and frowns. "I wonder if the person who left the note also took Bob's mice."

Ah. I bet Maya took the mice so she could feed the skink and the lizards.

"Probably," Mrs. Warner says. "We should call Bob and tell him."

"Yes," Mom agrees. "Do you have any idea who could have left the note? Any idea at all?"

"The note is typed." Mrs. Warner

hands the paper to Mom. "I don't think we'll ever know who left it."

I know who left it: Maya did.

"I don't mind keeping the lizards and the skink in the library, if it's okay with you?" Mrs. Warner says.

"It's fine with me," Mom says. "I just wish I knew who wrote this note. And I wish I knew what 'secret place' they were talking about."

I know where the secret place is: the furnace room.

I also know what Felix and Freckles are, and I know why Maya and Alex kept them hidden in the furnace room: because she wasn't allowed to keep them at home.

"I have a feeling we're never going to find answers to those questions," Mrs. Warner says.

"Probably not," Mom says.

Probably not, I agree. Because no one ever listens to the dog.

I think it's safe to say that I've solved the Case of the Library Monster now.

I wonder if there's anything else hidden in the furnace room? I wouldn't be surprised if there was... But that will have to be a case for another day.

Praise for The Buddy Files

"With twists and turns, humor, and a likable canine character, this series should find a wide fan base."—*Booklist*

"Readers should be drawn in by Buddy's exuberant voice." —*Publishers Weekly*

"Sweet and suspenseful." —*Kirkus Reviews*

The Buddy Files

Have you read all of Buddy's mysteries?

Turn the page and see!

THE BUDDY FILES:
THE CASE OF THE LOST BOY

King has a very big mystery to solve. His family is missing, and he's been put in the **P-O-U-N-D**. Why doesn't his beloved human (Kayla) come to get him? When King is adopted by Connor and his mom, things get more confusing. The new family calls him Buddy! And just as Connor and Buddy start to get acquainted, Connor disappears! With some help from his friend Mouse (a very large dog) and the mysterious Cat with No Name, Buddy shows what a smart, brave dog can do.

HC 978-0-8075-0910-4 • $14.99
PB 978-0-8075-0932-6 • $4.99

#2

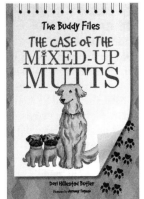

The Buddy Files

THE CASE OF THE
MIXED-UP
MUTTS

Dori Hillestad Butler
Pictures by Jeremy Tugeau

THE BUDDY FILES:
THE CASE OF THE
MIXED-UP MUTTS

Buddy was adopted from the
P-o-U-N-D and he likes his new
family, but he's still searching for
Kayla and her dad—his first family.
What has happened to them? He
hopes to solve that mystery soon,
but right now he's got another
urgent case—two dogs, Muffin and
Jazzy, have been switched! How
can Buddy get poor Muffin and
Jazzy back to their real owners?
HC 978-0-8075-0911-1 • $14.99
PB 978-0-8075-0933-3 • $4.99

#3

THE BUDDY FILES: THE CASE OF THE MISSING FAMILY

Buddy has settled in with his adopted family, but he's never given up on finding his beloved human, Kayla, and his first family. One night he sees people taking things out of Kayla's old house and loading them into a van. What's up? Though his friend Mouse advises against it, in the middle of the night Buddy decides to make a daring move, leaving everything he knows behind. Dori Butler's third case in *The Buddy Files* will entertain and satisfy the many fans of this brave, funny, and loyal dog.

HC 978-0-8075-0912-8 • $14.99
PB 978-0-8075-0934-0 • $4.99

THE BUDDY FILES: THE CASE OF THE LIBRARY MONSTER

Buddy is starting his work as a therapy dog at Four Lakes Elementary School, where Connor attends and Mom is the principal. On his very first day, he accidentally knocks down a little kid on the playground, convincing the first grade teacher that school is no place for a dog. Then the fire alarm goes off. The school is evacuated, but there's no fire...it's a false alarm. Who could have set it?

HC 978-0-8075-0913-5 • $14.99
PB 978-0-8075-0935-7 • $4.99